Nine Days to Christmas

Also by Marie Hall Ets

MISTER PENNY

THE STORY OF A BABY

IN THE FOREST

OLEY: THE SEA MONSTER

LITTLE OLD AUTOMOBILE

MR. T. W. ANTHONY WOO

ANOTHER DAY

PLAY WITH ME

MISTER PENNY'S RACE HORSE

COW'S PARTY

Nine Days to Christmas

By Marie Hall Ets and Aurora Labastida
Illustrated by Marie Hall Ets

The Viking Press · New York

To all the little Mexican friends and
relatives who helped us make this book

Copyright © 1959 by Marie Hall Ets and Aurora Labastida
First published in 1959 by The Viking Press, Inc.
625 Madison Avenue, New York 22, N.Y.
Published simultaneously in Canada by
The Macmillan Company of Canada Limited
Second printing April 1960
Third printing November 1960
Fourth printing October 1961
Fifth printing January 1964

LITHOGRAPHED IN U.S.A. BY AFFILIATED LITHOGRAPHERS

Christmas was coming. Ceci knew, for all the children were talking about it. Then one day she heard her mother and aunts making plans for the *posadas*—the special Christmas parties. Each night for nine nights before Christmas there would be a posada, and each night at a different house.

"Let us have the first one at our house," her mother said, "for now that Ceci is old enough to go to kindergarten I think she is old enough to stay up for the posadas—and old enough to have one of her own."

Ceci hardly could believe it—that *she* was going to have a posada!

"And will I have a *piñata*?" she asked. She was thinking of all the wonderful piñatas that hung outside the factory where they are made. She knew that piñatas were only paper with clay pots inside, but they all *seemed* alive.

6

"Whoever heard of a posada with no piñata?" Aunt Matilde laughed, giving a twitch to one of Ceci's tiny braids.

"But *will* I have one?" Ceci asked her mother again.

"You wait and see, Ceci," said her mother. "You wait and see."

7

The next day, as on every other day, Ceci's big brother, Salvador, left her at the kindergarten gate on his way to school. And as on every day Ceci watered the flowers in the big garden, and danced in a circle, and painted pictures. But at noon, just before it was time for the

children to run to the gate to see who was waiting for them, Ceci's teacher called her group together under the pepper tree and gave each child a pretty candy and said good-by. For, unlike other days, today was the last day of school.

"Hurrah! Hurrah!" said Salvador as he and Ceci walked home together. "No more school until February!"

Salvador was happy that school was over. Now he could play baseball with the other boys, and watch television at his grandmother's, and play his guitar. But Ceci was sad. She loved her kindergarten and didn't know what she could do at home while she waited for her Christmas posada.

"How long will I have to wait?" she asked Salvador.

"Wait for what?" he asked.

"For my posada!" said Ceci.

"Till nine days before Christmas," he said. "Twenty-one days."

The next morning, before anyone else in the house was up, Ceci was out watching María, their servant, sweep the front sidewalk. "Is today the day of my posada?" she asked.

"Not yet, Ceci." María laughed. "Not yet!"

Later Ceci went with María down the street to where two old women were selling *tortillas*, corn-flour pancakes. The women were slapping the dough between their hands and throwing the cakes on a sheet of hot iron to bake. Other servant girls were buying tortillas already made, but María just bought some dough. María knew how to slap the pancakes herself.

10

As they came back past their corner they stopped again
and María bought the morning newspaper for Ceci's father.

After breakfast, when her father left for the office, Ceci ran to the gate with him and kissed him good-by. Then she went in and watched her mother bathe the baby. When the baby was dressed her mother let Ceci hold him for just a minute. But then her mother took him away and put him in his crib to sleep.

"Let me go with you," said Ceci, when she saw that her mother was getting ready to go to market.

"Oh no, Ceci," said her mother. "You're too little to go to market!"

So Ceci picked up her favorite doll, Gabina, to play with. "No one will *ever* take me to market!" she told Gabina. "But someday I will go! And I will take you too, Gabina! Do you want to go to market?" And because Gabina's head was loose, Ceci only had to give her a little shake to make her nod yes.

13

When her mother had gone Ceci sat down by the gate and watched what was happening in the street.

Beautiful automobiles raced by.

An old man too poor to have shoes went by. He was carrying such a heavy load on his back that he almost had to run to keep from falling.

Two village women went by with babies on their backs and their arms full of flowers for the market.

The milkman came with his little cart and stood behind the wall where Ceci couldn't see him. But when he rang the bell María came running out and bought three bottles of milk.

Then came a man selling baskets and brooms, and a man selling birds.

Where are my birds? thought Ceci. And she got up and ran back to the patio to see if they were outside.

They were. And there on the wall between her patio and the neighbor's patio was the neighbor's big cat—the one with no tail!

"María! María!" called Ceci. "The cat's after my birds again!"
So María came out and carried the cage back into the kitchen.

On Sunday, María went home to her village. And after mass Ceci and her family went to the park. Ceci loved all the flowers and fountains. But best of all she liked the ducks on the lake. When she had

finished her picnic on the grass, she took some cookies and ran down
by the water to feed the ducks. "I'm going to have a posada," she told
them. "And maybe I'll have a piñata."

The next day when Ceci was supposed to be taking a nap she was thinking of the ducks. I wish I was a duck, she thought. I wish I was a duck sitting on the water! I wonder how it would feel? And she climbed out of bed and ran to the bathroom. She filled the tub half full of water, then took off her clothes and climbed in.

"Oh! Oh! Oh!" she gasped, for the water was so cold it took her breath away. She sat down in it anyway and tried to quack, but her teeth chattered so much that it sounded more like a little girl crying. It wasn't any fun at all to be a duck!

"Ceci! Ceci!" called her mother, running from the kitchen. "What's the matter? Where are you?"

And when her mother came into the bathroom and saw Ceci blue with cold she said, "Ceci! What under the sun are you doing in that ice-cold water!" She lifted Ceci out and started rubbing her with a big bath towel. "Don't you know that I always have to light the heater and warm the water before you can take a bath!"

"I wasn't taking a bath," said Ceci. "I just wanted to be a duck." And she began to cry.

"Oh, Ceci, *little one!*" said her mother, hugging her close. "I wasn't scolding! I was just frightened. I'm afraid you've caught cold!"

But even after she was dressed in warm clothes and sitting in the sun in the patio Ceci was still sad. She couldn't forget the poor ducks and how cold they must be out there in the park.

20

"Ceci!" called María, running for the garbage pail. "There's the
bell-ringer! Hurry and you can go with me!"

Meeting on the corner and waiting for the garbage truck was the
happiest time of the day for the servant girls on the street. As they

laughed and pinched her cheek and asked about her first posada. Ceci forgot about the poor ducks.

"And what kind of piñata will you have, Ceci?" asked one.

"I don't know," said Ceci. "I don't know if I will have one."

Then one morning Ceci's mother called her in earlier than usual to comb her hair. "I have a surprise for you, Ceci," she said. "Can you guess what it is?"

Ceci guessed a new doll, then a new dress. But it was neither of these.

"Guess again," said her mother.

"Is it—is it—*can it be a piñata*?" asked Ceci.

"That's it," said her mother. "It's your piñata."

"Oh, where is it?" asked Ceci. "I want to see it!"

"It isn't here," said her mother. "Today I'm taking you to market with me so you can choose your own piñata."

Before her mother could finish braiding and tying the yarn in her hair Ceci was pulling away. Then off she ran to tell Gabina. "I'm going to have a piñata, Gabina!" she said. "And I'm going to market to choose it myself! I'll choose the most beautiful piñata in the world! And it will be yours too, Gabina. Do you want to go to market with me?" And without waiting for Gabina to nod yes, Ceci grabbed up her doll and a little shawl and ran back to the kitchen to wait for her mother.

"Are we going to the big new supermarket?" Ceci asked her mother as they waited on the corner for the bus.

"No, Ceci," said her mother. "For your piñata and other things we need for a posada we must go to an old Mexican market."

24

As they entered the Christmastime market Ceci stopped still. Fairies and goblins must have been here in the night, she thought. How else could it be so beautiful! There were candies and toys and

sparklers and painted clay figures of Joseph and Mary and the donkey, and little lambs and cows. But Ceci didn't look long at these, for on ahead, swinging and turning in the wind, were the piñatas.

And since her mother had stopped to buy candles and other things, Ceci went on, nearer and nearer the piñatas. There were hundreds of piñatas. ENORMOUS piñatas. BIG piñatas. And little piñatas. And as Ceci entered the world of the piñatas they all came to life and greeted her.

"Welcome! Welcome, little girl!" they said. "Do you want to know us better?" And they turned around this way and that, so she could see them from all sides.

"Why don't you hang your doll up here with us?" said a gay parrot.

"That doll would enjoy dancing in the wind before she is broken."

"Broken! Oh, no!" said Ceci, holding Gabina closer. "This is a *real* doll! This is not a piñata!"

"What are you doing here, little girl, all by yourself?" asked a wise owl.

"I am choosing one of you for my first posada," said Ceci.

Now when the other piñatas heard this they all started calling to her, asking her to choose them. For wonderful things often happened to piñatas chosen by little girls for their first posadas. That was because the little girls loved them.

"Take me!" said one. "I am little and you can carry me better!"

"Take me!" said an elephant. "I am big and can hold more fruit."

"Baa-baa!" said a lamb. "Take me! I am soft and white and have a nice bell you can keep for yourself when I am broken!"

Ceci didn't know which one to choose! So she went on. Suddenly she stopped. For there, up above the other piñatas, was a big, shining gold star. "Oh!" said Ceci. "You're the most beautiful piñata in the world!"

But the star said nothing. It just kept shining and turning about for her to see.

"Ceci!" called her mother. "You've gone too far! Wait for me!"

Now when Ceci's mother came near, all the piñatas were hanging in silence again. And Ceci could hear the voices of many people selling and buying things for the

Christmas posadas. "Which piñata do you want, Ceci?" asked her mother. "Have you decided?"

Ceci looked back at the other piñatas. She loved them all, but she could have only one. So she pointed to the star.

"Oh, what a beautiful one, Ceci!" said her mother. "It's the star that showed the Wise Men where to find the baby Jesus."

So they bought the big star and carried it home in a taxi.

And the next day when Ceci woke up, she didn't have to ask—she *knew*! It was the day she had been waiting for, the day of her posada!

Early in the morning her mother and María filled cornhusks with sweet corn-flour pudding mixed with raisins and packed them into kettles to steam. Then they colored fruit juice with bright red flowers from the market. Ceci was helping them fill little toys with candy when her father called from the patio that he and Salvador were almost ready for the piñata. Her father was holding the ladder and Salvador was stretching ropes between two trees in the patio.

So María got the piñata and hung it between two chairs in the kitchen, and Ceci filled it all by herself. She put in big juicy oranges, and tiny sweet lemons, and peanuts, and candies wrapped in pretty papers, and red-and-white sugar canes. Then she went and watched while her father and Salvador tied the filled piñata to the rope in the patio and pulled it way up into the air.

"Look, Ceci," said Salvador, pulling on the end of the rope that hung down by the jacaranda tree.

34

"This is the way we will pull your piñata up and down, to fool the children when they are blindfolded and trying to hit it."

"But I don't want them to hit it!" said Ceci.

"I don't want anyone to break my piñata!"

"What kind of posada will it be if no one breaks the piñata?"
Salvador laughed. "Piñatas are made to be broken."

Soon after dark, when all the guests had arrived, Ceci—who had
dressed up in her village costume, because she liked that better than
her other clothes—and her cousin Manuel led the procession which

starts every posada. Carrying Joseph and Mary and the donkey, they walked slowly around the patio. And everyone else followed with lighted candles, singing the song of the Holy Pilgrims.

Soon they came to a closed door at the side of the house and Ceci went up and knocked. At first the people behind the door sang back, "No. There's no room in the inn!" But in the end the door was opened and everyone sang, "Come in, Holy Pilgrims!"

So Ceci and Manuel went in and left Joseph and Mary and the donkey on a table. Then they ran back out to the patio.

Now the other children started shouting and singing, "Go on, Ceci, don't delay! Bring the toys of candy on a tray!"

So Ceci and her mother and María passed the big trays and gave everyone a toy filled with candy.

Ceci's piñata, in the middle of the patio, shone like a real star over their heads as the children ran from one side to the other, shooting firecrackers and waving sparklers. "I don't want gold!" they began to sing. "I don't want silver! What I want is to break the piñata!"

So Salvador brought out a long club and a big hand-kerchief and asked Aunt Matilde and Uncle Pepe to blind-fold the children and whirl them around, while *he* held the rope by the tree to pull the piñata up and down. Then there was great excitement, for everyone wanted to be first to try to break the piñata.

The small children just hit the air and made everyone laugh. But
the older ones started hitting the piñata. "Blindfold Ceci!" called
Manuel. "You try, Ceci! It's fun!" But Ceci wouldn't try, or watch.

42

She went and stood behind the tree near Salvador. "Don't let them hit it!" she said. "Don't let them break my piñata!"

But Salvador, laughing with the others, paid no attention to her.

43

Suddenly there was a crash. Then came shouting and the sound of children scrambling over one another as they tried to grab the good

44

things that were rolling around on the ground. *They've broken it!*
thought Ceci, but she didn't move or look. She just stood there

listening. And as she listened she heard a voice up in the branches whispering, "Ceci! Ceci!"

And there, just above the tree, was the brightest star she had ever seen. "Don't cry, Ceci," it whispered. "Look! Because a little girl chose me for her first posada, I'm a *real* star now!"

And as Ceci watched, the star flew up to the sky.

No one can ever break it now! she thought. *And it will always be mine, mine and Gabina's.* Suddenly Ceci disappeared around the corner of the house. A minute later she was back, with Gabina in her arms.

"Look, Gabina!" she said. "They couldn't break it because it was *real!* They only broke the pot inside. And *we—*

we have given the world a new star for Christmas. *Our* star, Gabina! Can you see how it's blinking just at us?"

And Gabina looked and she nodded her head three times.